The Writing of Middle Earth

ᛟᛗ · ᛈᚱᛁᛏᛁᚻᚷ · ᚠᚹ · ᛗᛁᛝᛝᛚᛗ · ᛗᚨᚱᛟ

ᚷᛁ · ᛟᛏᛁᚱᛁᚷ · ᚪᚲ · ᛒᛁᚠᚠᚻᚾ · ᚻᚾᛏᚱ

FH ᚱᚲᛁᚱᛁᚹ ᚾᚢ ᚷᛁᛏᛏᚷᚻ ᚻᛞᚲF

þ᛫ ᴅyıpıᴃ þ᛫ ᴃıᴘᴣᴄᴧ ᴧᴄyb

þ᛫ ᴅypᴃ̈ þ᛫ ᴃᴘ̇ᴄ íẙb

By

HL Fourie

Table of Contents

Introduction

Welcome to the Writing of Middle Earth. You've read The Hobbit and seen the movies. Do you remember Thror's map with the runish lettering? Well this book explains all about the rune script of The Hobbit as well as the other scripts used by the Elves and the Dwarves.

Tolkien not only invented Hobbit runes but several other scripts and languages as well. Tolkien was a philologist, an expert in the study of languages, so he was able to create several languages and also describe how they evolved through the ages of Middle Earth.

The languages that Tolkien mentioned in the sagas of Middle Earth included the following:

- Quenya or High Elven is the ancient speech of the Noldor Elves. This is also called the Ancient Tongue or Valinorean.

- Sindarin, spoken by the Grey (or Sindar) Elves, was derived from Quenya during the time the Grey Elves lived in Beleriand.

- Khuzdul, spoken by the Dwarves.

- Westron or Common Speech which was spoken by many groups as a second language. This is represented by English.

- Black Speech, spoken by Sauron and his Orcs.

In *The Hobbit*, the author J.R.R. Tolkien introduced Hobbit runes. In *The Lord of the Rings* books he also described several other languages and scripts that he had invented for Middle Earth. The Elvish languages used a script called Tengwar that dated from the First Age of Middle Earth. Tengwar was used to write Quenya and Sindarin, which are both languages of the Elves. The inscription on the One Ring was written in a form of Tengwar called Black Script. Tengwar characters had curved strokes and were usually written with pen and ink.

Another script mentioned by Tolkien was Cirth (pronounced 'kirth'), which was originally invented by the Sindar Elves. The elf Daeron then used these old runes to develop a new script that was similar to Tengwar in the way the sounds of the language were mirrored by the shapes of the runes. This was called Certhas Daeron, the alphabet of Daeron. The Noldor Elves then expanded it into Angerthas Daeron to be used for their own language, Quenya, as well as the languages of Men. These runes were straight and angular for ease of cutting or scratching on stone, wood or metal. Angerthas Daeron was also adopted by the Dwarves for writing their Khuzdul language.

There was also another script called the Runes of Gondolin that was used by the Elves, about which little is known.

This book will teach you the alphabets of these different scripts and how to interpret the rune and Tengwar inscriptions that appear in Tolkien's books. You will even learn how to write your own name in these scripts. It's easy and fun, so let's get started.

Hobbit Runes

Hobbit runes first appear on Thror's Map in *The Hobbit*. They are very similar to old Anglo-Saxon runes. This ancient alphabet was called Futhark (or Futhorc) for its first six runes: f, u, th, a, r, and k. Tolkien said that the runes he described in *The Hobbit* represented those used by the Dwarves. Those runes are called Cirth runes and will be covered in a later chapter.

Rune Alphabet

Let's start with the rune alphabet shown below. This table shows the Hobbit runes for each letter of the English alphabet as well as the name of each rune. As you can see, all the letters in our alphabet except 'q' have a matching rune. For 'q' you can use either 'k' or 'cw' instead.

A	ash	ᚠ
B	birch	ᛒ
C	care	ᚲ
D	day	ᛞ
E	elm	ᛗ
F	fire	ᚹ
G	gift	ᚷ
H	hail	ᚻ

Letter	Word	Rune
I	ice	ᛁ
J		ᛃ
K	kin	ᚻ
L	land	ᚱ
M	man	ᛗ
N	need	ᛏ
O	ox	ᛟ
P	pine	ᛈ
R	road	ᚱ
S	sun	ᚺ
T	tongue	ᛏ
U	urn	ᚢ
V		ᚢ
W	wine	ᚹ
X		ᛉ
Y	yew	ᛇ
Z	zinc	ᛣ

There are similarities between our English alphabet and the Hobbit rune alphabet. This is because Tolkien derived the Hobbit runes from the old Anglo-Saxon futhark alphabet. See how B, H, I, R, S, and T are similar to ᛒ, ᚻ, ᛁ, ᚱ, ᚺ, and ᛏ. There is no lowercase in Hobbit runes.

In addition to the basic alphabet, there are some letter clusters that are represented as a single rune. It's a shortcut way of writing two letters as one. These are:

th	thorn	ᚦ
st	stone	ᛥ
ng	anger	ᛝ
ee	eel	ᛟ
ea	ear	ᛠ

Names of Dwarfs

Now let's start with the name of a very well-known dwarf, Thorin, the leader of a band of adventurers on the journey to Smaug's lair. You write Thorin like this ᚦᚩᚱᛁᚾ.

Notice that the rune ᚦ is used for the letters 'Th' of Thorin.

Now for the rest of the dwarves from Thorin's band.

Balin	ᛒᚪᛚᛁᚾ
Bifur	ᛒᛁᚹᚢᚱ
Bofur	ᛒᚩᚹᚢᚱ
Bombur	ᛒᚩᛗᛒᚢᚱ
Dori	ᛞᚩᚱᛁ
Nori	ᚾᚩᚱᛁ
Ori	ᚩᚱᛁ
Dwalin	ᛞᚹᚪᛚᛁᚾ

5

Fili	ᚹᛁᛚᛁ
Kili	ᚺᛁᛚᛁ
Gloin	ᚷᛚᛟᛁᚾ
Oin	ᛟᛁᚾ

Bilbo would be written as ᛒᛁᛚᛒᛟ and Gandalf as ᚷᚨᚾᛞᚨᛚᚠ. However, the name that Dwarfs of *The Hobbit* gave to Gandalf was Tharkun, spelled in runish as ᚦᚨᚱᚺᚢᚾ.

Thror's Map

Thror's map appears in the first pages of *The Hobbit*. Thorin had the map made by his grandfather, Thror, and so knew the way to The Lonely Mountain where the dragon, Smaug, had hidden treasure. First let's look at the points of the compass on the map so we can get oriented and find our way. You can see the letters ᛏ, ᚼ, ᛗ and ᚹ which of course mean North, South, East and West. It's important to notice that the map in *The Hobbit* is oriented so that North is to the left of the map. See if you can find a clue to where Durin's Door may be located.

Now let's look at those runish words that appear on the left side of Thror's map.

ᚹᛁᚾᛗ · ᚹᛟᛏ · ᚺᛁᚷᚺ · ᚦᛗ · ᚾᚹᚱ ·

Five   feet   high   the   door

Notice that the rune ᛉ is used for 'ee' in feet, and ᚦ is used for 'th' in the word 'the'. The rest of the sentence is:

ᚠᛏᚾ · ᚦᚱᛦ · ᛗᚠᛘ · ᛈᚠᚱᚻ · ᚠᛒᚱᛗᚠᚢᛏ ⁚
and   three may   walk   abreast

It is signed with Thror's initials ᚦᚦ which stand for Thror Thrain's son. Thror is written ᚦᚱᚠᚱ in Hobbit runes.

You can see that each word is separated by a dot, and three dots are used as a period at the end of a sentence. Notice where the finger is pointing on the map; that's another clue to finding Durin's Door.

Now let's look at the other runish words on the map with their meanings. These are the moon letters that Elrond was able to read on midsummer's eve by the light of the crescent moon.

ᚢᛏᚠᛏᚾ · ᛒᛘ · ᚦᛗ · ᚷᚱᛗᚻ · ᚢᛏᚠᛏᛗ
Stand   by   the   grey   stone

ᚹᚾᛗᛏ · ᚦᛗ · ᚦᚱᚾᚢᚾ · ᚻᛏᛈᚴᚻᚢ ·
when   the   thrush   knocks

ᚠᛏᚾ · ᚦᛗ · ᚢᛗᛏᛏᛁᛉ · ᚢᚾᛏ ·
and   the   setting   sun

ᚹᛁᚦ · ᚦᛗ · ᚴᚠᚢᛏ · ᚴᛁᚷᚾᛏ ·

7

with the   last   light

ᚠᚹ · ᛞᚢᚱᛁᛏᚻ · ᚾᚠᛗ ·
of   Durin's   Day

ᚹᛁᚱᚱ · ᚻᚾᛁᛏᛗ · ᚢᛈᚠᛏ ·
will   shine   upon

ᚦᛗ · ᚻᛗᛘᚾᚠᚱᛗ ᛬
the   keyhole.

Look at the map again and see if you can find the ᚾ on the western slope of The Lonely Mountain (Mount Erebor), which marks the location of Durin's Door.

The Jacket Cover of The Hobbit

There are also runes written on the jacket cover of *The Hobbit*. Let's decipher them.

ᚦᛗ · ᚾᚠᛒᛒᛁᛏ · ᚠᚱ ·
The Hobbit   or

ᚦᛗᚱᛗ · ᚠᛏᚾ · ᛒᚠᛦᚻ · ᚠᚷᚠᛁᛏ ᛬
there   and   back   again

ᛒᛗᛁᛏᚷ · ᚦᛗ · ᚱᛗᛦᚠᚱᚾ ·

being   the   record

ᚠᚹ · ᚠ · ᛗᛏᚱᚻ · ᛁᚠᚢᚱᛏᛗᛗ ·
of   a   year's   journey

ᛒᛗ · ᛒᛁᚷᛒᚠ · ᛒᚠᚷᚷᛁᛏᚻ · ᚠᚹ · ᚻᚠᛒᛒᛁᛏᚠᛏ ⁚
By   Bilbo   Baggins   of   Hobbiton.

ᚲᚠᛗᚲᛁᚷᛗᛗ · ᚹᚱᚠᛗ · ᚻᛁᚻ · ᛗᛗᚠᚠᛁᚱᚻ ·
compiled   from   his   memoirs

ᛒᛗ · ᛁ·ᚱ·ᚱ· ᛏᚠᚷᚻᛁᛗᛏ ⁚
by   J.R.R.   Tolkien.

ᚠᛏᛗ · ᚲᚢᛒᚷᚢᚻᛗᛗ · ᛒᛗ ·
and   published   by

ᚻᚠᚢᚷᚻᛏᚠᛏ · ᛗᛁᚹᚹᚷᛁᛏ· ᚠᛏᛗ · ᚲᚠ ⁚
Houghton   Mifflin   and   Co.

Names

Writing names using Hobbit runes is easy. Simply look up the letters for the name using the Hobbit Rune alphabet. Here are some examples:

Garth   ᚷᚠᚱᚦ

Elizabeth	ᛗᛚᛁᛌᛒᛖᚦ
Earnest	ᚣᚱᛂᛗᛞ
Judith	ᛏᚢᛞᛁᚦ
Smaug	ᛋᛗᛆᚢᚷ

Letter to Mrs. Farrer

Tolkien wrote a letter to a close friend of his, a Mrs. Farrer, in Hobbit Runes. This letter can be found in the book *The Letters of J.R.R. Tolkien* edited by Humphrey Carpenter. Here is the first sentence of that letter.

ᛞᚣᚱ·ᛗᚱᛋ·ᚠᚨᚱᚱᛗᚱ·ᚠᚣ·ᛚᚨᚦᚱᛋᛗ·

Dear Mrs. Farrer,   Of course

ᛁ·ᛈᛁᛚᛚ·ᛋᛁᚷᛂ·ᛗᚨᚦᚱ·ᛚᚨᚳᛗ·

I will   sign your   copy

ᚠᚣ·ᚦᛗ·ᚺᚨᛒᛁᛏᛝ

of the Hobbit.

Try writing a letter to a friend. For a summer project, try silk-screening your name in runes on a T-shirt.

Riddles

Here is a riddle in Hobbit Runes. See if you can figure it out; the answer is at the back of the book.

ᚠ·ᛒᚩᛉ·ᚹᛁᚦᚢᛏ·ᚻᛁᛝᛖᛋ·ᚳᛖᚣ·ᚩᚱ·ᛚᛁᛞ·

ᚣᛖᛏ·ᚷᚩᛚᛞᛖᚾ·ᛏᚱᛖᚪᛋᚢᚱᛖ·ᛁᚾᛋᛁᛞᛖ·ᛁᛋ·ᚻᛁᛞ⁝

Cirth

History of Cirth

The Elves initially created Cirth during the First Age. Daeron, the Elvish lore-master and minstrel to King Thingol, organized the runish alphabet into a more systematic alphabet which was to become known as Angerthas Daeron or the Alphabet of Daeron. The Noldor Elves further developed the Cirth. When Daeron revised the Cirth he arranged that the shapes of the runes have a regular relationship to that of corresponding Tengwar letters. A single Cirth rune is called a *certh,* derived from the Quenya word meaning 'to cut', signifying that these angular runes were cut or scratched into a writing surface such as stone or wood.

During the Second Age, the Dwarves of Moria came to hear of this runish alphabet and adopted it for themselves to write their Khuzdul language. The Dwarves made more changes to it and this slightly different Cirth alphabet was known as Angerthas Moria. This script is used on Balin's tomb in Moria.

Finally, during the Third Age, when the Dwarves were driven from Moria by the Balrog and Orc forces, they fled to The Lonely Mountain (Mount Erebor). The Dwarvish settlement at Erebor was founded in 1999 of the Third Age by Thráin I. The Dwarves of Erebor made additional changes to the Cirth to form Angerthas Erebor.

See Appendix E in the *The Fellowship of the Ring* for Tolkien's description of Cirth script.

Angerthas Daeron Alphabet

Table 1 shows the matching Angerthas Daeron rune for each letter of the English alphabet. As you can see, most of the letters in the English alphabet have a matching Cirth rune.

a	b	c	d	e	f	g	h
ᚾ	ᚱ	ᚡ	ᚠ	ᚺ	ᚴ	ᚡ	ᚦ

i	j	k	l	m	n	o	p
ᛁ	ᛕ	ᚡ	ᛏ	ᛒ	ᚠ	ᚠ	ᛈ

r	s	t	u	v	w	y	z
ᚲ	ᚦ᚜	ᚳ	ᛝ	ᛉ	ᛢ	ᚼ	ᛪ

Table 1: Angerthas Daeron Alphabet

There are some interesting aspects to this alphabet. There are no Angerthas Daeron runes for 'q' and 'x'. Instead 'k', 'kw' or 'cw' can be used for 'q', and 'ks' can be used for 'x'. The letters 'c' and 'k' share the same rune ᚡ so this rune should only be used where the hard 'c' as in 'cat' is needed. There are two different Cirth runes for the letter 's': ᚦ and ᚴ.

Angerthas Moria Alphabet

The Dwarves of Middle Earth heard about Angerthas Daeron and used it to create a slightly different version of their own called Angerthas Moria. Angerthas Moria was used by the Dwarves to write their own language Khuzdul. Balin's tomb in Khazad-dûm was inscribed with Angerthas Moria runes.

Table 2 shows the matching Angerthas Moria rune for each letter of the English alphabet. The Angerthas Moria runes h, j, n, r, s, and z differ from the Angerthas Daeron runes. There are no Angerthas Moria runes for 'q' and 'x'.

a	b	c	d	e	f	g	h
ᚻ	ᚱ	ᚢ	ᚠ	ᚺ	ᚣ	ᚤ	ᚦ

i	j	k	l	m	n	o	p
ᛁ	ᚲ	ᚢ	ᛏ	ᛒ	ᚣ	ᚪ	ᛈ

r	s	t	u	v	w	y	z
↑	ᚴ	ᚱ	ᚸ	ᚱ	ᚥ	ᚼ	ᛃ

Table 2: Angerthas Moria Alphabet

Here is how you would write the word 'Moria' using Angerthas Moria:

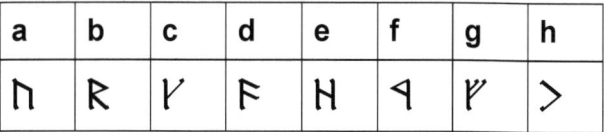

Angerthas Erebor Alphabet

Angerthas Erebor was derived from Angerthas Moria by the Dwarves at their settlement at Erebor.

Table 3 shows the matching Angerthas Erebor rune for each letter of the English alphabet. The Angerthas Erebor runes h, j, s, and z differ from the Angerthas Moria runes. There are no Angerthas Erebor runes for 'q' and 'x'. There are two different Angerthas Erebor runes for 'n': Y and Y.

a	b	c	d	e	f	g	h
ᚺ	ᚱ	ᚲ	ᚠ	ᚻ	ᚴ	ᛈ	ᛚ

i	j	k	l	m	n	o	p
ᛁ	ᚴ	ᚲ	ᛏ	ᛒ	ᚤᛉ	ᛚ	ᛈ

r	s	t	u	v	w	y	z
ᛏ	ᚷᚳ	ᛐ	ᚴ	ᛉ	ᛞ	ᚺ	ᛝ

Table 3: Angerthas Erebor Alphabet

There is a set of Cirth runes to represent doubled or long vowels. Long vowels are those in the words cake, mete, ride, poke and cute, as compared with short vowels in the words bat, met, bit, pot and cut.

ā	ē	ī	ō	ū
ᚻ	ᚼ	‖	ᛗ	ᛟ

Table 4: Cirth Long Vowels

For example the word 'book' would be written ᚱᛗᛌ.

The Cirth rune ᚼ represents the word 'and'.

Consonant Clusters

In addition there are some consonant clusters that are represented as a single Cirth rune. These are:

ch	sh	th	dh	zh	kh	gh	lh	rh
ᚲ	ᚾ	ᚱ	ᚴ	ᚳ	ᚣ	ᚤ	ᛏ	ᚵ

hw	kw	gw	khw	ghw	ngw	nw	nd	ng
ᚦ	ᚱ	ᚨ	ᚹ	ᚻ	ᛏ	ᛣ	ᚷ	ᚷᚯ

ps	ts	mb
ᚦ	ᛈ	ᛇ

Table 5: Cirth for Consonant Clusters

Here is how you would write the word 'Cirth' using Angerthas Moria: ᚲᛁᛏᛚ using the Cirth rune ᛏ for the 'th' sound.

The letter ᚲ was used by Gandalf to sign the letter to Frodo that he entrusted to Butterbur. It appears in the chapter 'Strider' in *The Fellowship of the Ring*. Gandalf is written as:

ᚲᚺᚷᚺᚻᛏᚦ

Cirth Punctuation

There is a set of vertical dots that may be used to separate words, sentences, paragraphs, and blocks of text.

Word separator	᛫
Period	᛬
Paragraph	᛬
Block of text	᛭

Table 6: Cirth Punctuation

You should now be able to read the title of this book written using Angerthas Moria alphabet.

᛬ ᛏᛁ ᛫ ᚢᛏᛁᚱᛟ ᛫ ᛚᚦ ᛫ ᛒᛁᚠᚠᛏᚺ ᛫ ᚺᚢᛏᛏ ᛬

Names in Cirth

Here are some examples of what Angerthas Moria script looks like for names of people and places of Middle Earth.

Balin	ᚱᚾᚻᛁᛦ
Bifur	ᚱᛁᛈᛇᛏ
Bofur	ᚱᚢᛈᛇᛏ
Bombur	ᚱᚢᛒᚱᛇᛏ
Dori	ᚠᚢᛏᛁ
Nori	ᛦᚢᛏᛁ
Ori	ᚢᛏᛁ
Dwalin	ᚠᛣᚾᚻᛁᛦ
Fili	ᛈᛁᚻᛁ
Kili	ᚳᛁᚻᛁ
Gloin	ᚳᛏᚢᛁᛦ
Oin	ᚢᛁᛦ
Gimli	ᚳᛁᛒᚻᛁ
Tharkun	ᛠᚾᛏᚳᛇᛦ
Khazaddûm	ᚳᚾᚢᚾᚠᚠᛟᛒ
Khuzdul	ᚳᛇᚢᚠᛇᛏ

See the use of the Cirth rune ᛠ in Tharkun (the Dwarves' name for Gandalf). Also notice the little vertical bar ᚳᛁ that follows the Cirth rune V in the Cirth words Khazad-dûm and Khuzdul. This adds an 'h' to these words.

The Lord of the Rings Title Page

The title page of *The Fellowship of the Ring* has the following Cirth script at the top of the page.

ᛂᚩᛁ·ᛏᛚᛏᚠ·ᛚᛃ·ᚩᛁ·ᛏᛁᚷᚲ

The Lord   of   the Rings

ᚱᛏᚻᛁᚲᚳᛏᚾᚸᚠ·ᚤᛏᛚᛒ·ᚩᛁ·ᛏᚻᚠ·ᚱᛉᛁᚸᛂ

translat(e)d   from   the red   book.

The word 'The' uses some unusual letters, the Cirth rune $\daleth$ shows that Tolkien intended the sound 'dh' to be used instead of 'th'. Also the rune t is used instead of H for the letter 'e'. In the word 'rings', the Cirth rune X is used instead of separate 'n' and 'g' runes. In the word 'of', the Cirth rune $\mathcal{R}$ is used for the 'ov' sound.

Balin's Tomb Inscription

Angerthas Moria script is used in the inscription on Balin's tomb in Moria. This appears at the end of the chapter 'A Journey in the Dark' in *The Fellowship of the Ring*.

ᚱᚾᚻᛁᛣ

Balin

ᚴᛣᛉᛁᛣᛉᛏ

Fundinul

ᛉᛁᚱᚾᚠ ᛣᛁᚾᛁᚾᚠᚠᛉᛒᛉ

Uzbad   Khazaddûmu

The English translation of this is:

ᚱᚾᚻᛁᛣ ᚲᛁᛣ ᛚᚫ ᚴᛣᛉᛁᛣ

Balin   son of   Fundin

ᛏᛚᛏᚠ ᛚᚫ ᚴᛣᛉᛁᛣ

Lord   of   Moria

Examples

Here are some additional examples of Angerthas Moria script.

Orcrist	ᛚᛏᚤᛏᛁᚲᛚ
Orc Hunter	ᛚᛏᚤ ᛚᛩᚤᛚᚻᛏ
Glamdring	ᚤᚻᚾᛒᚠᛏᛁᛟ

Cirth Numbers

Tolkien also gave some examples of Cirth numbers.

1	2	3	4	5	6
ᛁ	ᚥ	ᚦ	ᛛ	ᚤ	ᛁᛁᛁᛁᛁᛁ

Table 7: Cirth Numbers

Runes of Gondolin

History

Very little is known of the Runes of Gondolin. J.R.R. Tolkien wrote of these runes on a slip of paper, a photocopy of which Christopher Tolkien sent to Paul Nolan Hyde in February 1992, and which was published, together with an extensive analysis, in the Summer 1992 issue of *Mythlore*, the journal of the Mythopoeic Society.

Gondolin, also called the Hidden Kingdom, was built in secret by the Elf king Turgon during the First Age. It was eventually destroyed by Orcs and Balrogs in the last days of the First Age. Presumably, these runes were used by the Elven inhabitants of Gondolin.

Alphabet

Table 1 shows the matching rune for each letter of the Latin alphabet. There are no runes for the letters 'c', 'q' and 'x'. For a soft 'c' use 's', and for a hard 'c' use 'k'. For 'q' and 'x' use 'kw' and 'ks' respectively.

a	b	d	e	f	g	h	i
▶	W	↑	H	V	℞	ı	ǀ

j	k	l	m	n	o	p	r
⚵	ᚦ	X	⚼	ᚱ	ᚴ	V	K

s	t	u	v	w	y	z
<	ᚥ	◊	ᚤ	⚼	ᚴ	⚭

Table 1: Runes of Gondolin

There is also a set of Runes for some consonant clusters. The cluster 'th' would be used as in the word 'thin' and the cluster 'dh' would be used as in the word 'then'. The cluster 'ch' has the sound as in 'church' and the cluster 'kh' has the sound as in 'Bach'.

ch	dh	kh	mh	nh	rh	sh	th
ᚳ	ᚹ	ᚺ	⚼	ᚱ	ᚷ	ᚻ	ᚠ

wh	zh	hy	ks	ng
⚼	↓	ᚼ	ᚲ	ᚱ

Table 2: Consonant Clusters

Long vowels have their own set of runes.

ā	ē	ī	ō	ū
ᛗ	ᚺ	ᛏ	ᚱ	◊

Table 3: Long Vowels

Names

Here are some examples of what this script looks like for names of people and places in the neighbourhood of Gondolin.

Gondolin	ᛒᚢᚱᛏᚢᚷᛁᚥ
Turgon	ᚲᛟᚲᛒᚢᚱ
Hithlum	ᛁᚠᚷᛟᚥ
Mithrim	ᚥᛁᚠᚲᛁᚥ
Tol Sirion	ᚲᚢᚷ ᚲᛁᚲᛁᚢᚱ
Echoriath	ᚺᚦᚢᚲᛁᚦᚠ

Here is the title of the book written in the Runes of Gondolin.

ᚠᚺ ᚥᚲᛁᚲᛁᚥ ᚢᚥ ᚥᛁᛏᛏᚷᚺ ᚺᚦᚲᚠ

Tengwar

History of Tengwar

Tengwar was the script used to write several Elvish languages of Middle Earth. Tengwar had its origins in Sarati, which was a script created by Rúmil of Tirion, a Noldor Elf. Fëanor, who was known as the greatest of the Noldor Elves, invented Tengwar, which was a more systematic method of representing different sounds. He was the eldest son of Finwë. Fëanor created the far-seeing *palantiri* and also captured the light of the Two Trees of Valinor, Telperion and Laurelin, within three jewels known as the Silmarils.

Tengwar was used to write Quenya or High-Elven, spoken by the Noldor or Deep Elves. Later it was used to write Sindarin, spoken by the Grey Elves who lived with King Thingol at Doriath. There was also a form for the Black Speech of Sauron as well as for Westron, the language of the Men of Middle Earth. Each form has a slightly different alphabet and rules about how to write the vowels.

See Appendix E in the *The Fellowship of the Ring* for Tolkien's description of Tengwar script. It should be noted that there are many variations on how to write Tengwar in the examples that are found in the writings of J.R.R. Tolkien and his son, Christopher Tolkien. This chapter presents one way of writing Tengwar with some of the options that are used by J.R.R. Tolkien and Christopher Tolkien.

Tengwar Letter Shapes

The word Tengwa means 'letter' or 'character'. Each Tengwar character is called a *tengwa* and the plural is *tengwar*. There are about 36 Tengwar characters, 24 of which have a similar construction. These all have a stem called a *telco* and a bow called a *luva,* as shown below for the tinco *tengwa.*

stem (telco) $\longrightarrow$ p $\longleftarrow$ bow (luva)

The Tengwar letters that use the same stem and bow construction differ in the following ways:

- The bow could be open or closed.

- The bow could be on the left or right of the stem.

- There could be a single or double bow.

- The stem could be the same height as the bow.

- The stem could extend above the bow.

- The stem could extend below the bow.

The shape of a Tengwar letter was used to represent its sound:

- If the bow was to the right of the stem and opened downward, then the sounds were made with the front of the mouth, like t, d, p, or f.

- If the bow was to the left of the stem and opened upward, then the sounds were made with the back of the mouth, like ch, k, j, g, hw, or gw.

- A single bow indicated non-nasal sounds like f, t, or r.

- A double bow indicated nasal sounds like m, n, nd, or mp.

Tengwar Alphabet

The different stem and bow shapes result in the 24 primary Tengwar letters shown below in Table 1. Tolkien organized these Tengwar into a table of four columns or series (called *téma*) and six rows according to the kinds of sounds they make.

	I		II		III		IV	
	Tincotéma		Parmatéma		Calmatéma		Quessetéma	
1	ᴘ	tinco	ᴘ	parma	�q	calma	ᴨ	quesse
2	ᴘ͘	ando	ᴘ͘	umbar	ᴄq	anga	ᴨ͘	ungwe
3	ᴎ	thule	ᴎ	formen	ᴅ	harma	ᴅ	hwesta
4	ᴎ͘	anto	ᴎ͘	ampa	ᴄᴅ	anca	ᴄᴅ͘	unque
5	ᴍ	númen	ᴍ	malta	ᴄᴜ	noldo	ᴄᴜ͘	nwalme
6	ᴨ	óre	ᴅ	vala	ᴜ	anna	ᴜ͘	vilya

Table 1: Primary Tengwar letters

The sounds of the Tincotéma series are made with the tip of the tongue against or near to the teeth. These sounds are called the dentals. These are sounds like t, d, th.

The sounds of the Parmatéma series are made with the lips. These include sounds like p, f, m, v.

The sounds of the Calmatéma series are made with the tongue close to the roof of the mouth.

The sounds of the Quessetéma series are made with the back of the tongue close to the roof of the mouth with the lips slightly pursed.

There are 12 additional characters shown below in Table 2.

y	rómen	ỵ	arda	ᴄ	lambe	ᴢ	alda
6	silme	?	silme nuquerna	8	áze, esse	3	áze nuquerna
λ	hyarmen	ḓ	Hwesta sindarinwa	ʌ	yanta	o	úre

Table 2: Additional Tengwar letters

Let's go over the 36 *tengwar* in more detail.

p **tinco (1)** This was the Quenya word for 'metal' and had the sound 't'.

p **parma (2)** This was the Quenya word for 'book' and had the sound 'p'.

calma (3) This was the Quenya word for 'lamp' and had the sound 'ch'.

quesse (4) This was the Quenya word for 'feather' and had the sound 'kw'.

ando (5) This was the Quenya word for 'gate' and had the sound 'nd'. In Sindarin and other languages it would be used for the sound 'd'.

umbar (6) This was the Quenya word for 'fate' and represented the sound 'mb'. In Sindarin it has the sound 'b'. Umbar was also the name of the seaport at the southern end of the Bay of Belfalas that was settled by the Númenoreans during the Second Age.

anga (7) This was the Quenya word for 'iron' and represented the sound 'ng'. In Sindarin it had the sound 'g'. This is used in Sindarin names like Angmar (iron-home) and Angrenost (iron-citadel).

ungwe (8) This was the Quenya word for 'spider-web' and had a hard 'ngw' sound. In Sindarin it had a 'gw' sound.

thúle (9) This was the Quenya word for 'spirit' and had the sound 'th' or 's'. In Sindarin the sound was 'th'. This *tengwa* also has the Sindarin name Sûle meaning 'wind', as found in the name Amon Sûl 'Hill of Winds'.

b **formen (10)** This was the Quenya word for 'north' and had the sound 'f'.

d **harma (11)** This was the Quenya word for 'treasure' and had the sound 'h'. This *tengwa* also had the name Aha meaning 'rage'.

d **hwesta (12)** This was the Quenya word for 'breeze' and had the sound 'hw'.

ʰɔ **anto (13)** This was the Quenya word for 'mouth' and had the sound 'nt'. In Sindarin the sound was 'dh'.

ʰɔ **ampa (14)** This was the Quenya word for 'hook' and had the sound 'mp'. In Sindarin the sound was 'v'.

ɑd **anca (15)** This was the Quenya word for 'jaws' and had the sound 'nk'. In Sindarin the sound was 'zh'.

ɑ̣ **unque (16)** This was the Quenya word for 'hollow' and had the sound 'nkw'. In Sindarin the sound was 'gh'.

ᴅᴅ númen (17) This was the Quenya word for 'west' and had the sound 'n'.

ᴅᴅ malta (18) This was the Quenya word for 'gold' and had the sound 'm'.

ᴄᴄ noldo (19) This was the Quenya word for 'of the Noldor' and had the sound 'ng'.

ᴄᴄ nwalme (20) This was the Quenya word for 'torment' and had the sound 'nw'.

ᴅ óre (21) This was the Quenya word for 'heart' and had the sound 'r'. In Sindarin the sound it represented was 'n'.

ᴅ vala (22) This was the Quenya word for 'angelic power' and had the sound 'w'. In Sindarin the sound it represented was 'm'.

ᴄ anna (23) This was the Quenya word for 'gift' and had the sound 'y'.

ᴄ vilya (24) This was the Quenya word for 'sky' or 'air' and represented the sound 'r'.

ɣ **rómen (25)** This was the Quenya word for 'east' and had the sound 'r'.

ɣ **arda (26)** This was the Quenya word for 'region' or 'realm' and represented the sound 'rd' in Quenya and the sound 'rh' in Sindarin or Westron. Arda was the name that Ilúvatar, the Supreme Being of Middle Earth, gave to the World that he had created.

ᴄ **lambe (27)** This was the Quenya word for 'tongue' and had the sound 'l'.

ᴢ **alda (28)** This was the Quenya word for 'tree' and had the sound 'ld'. In Sindarin this *tengwa* stood for the sound 'lh'.

6 **silme (29)** This was the Quenya word for 'starlight' and had the sound 's'.

ᴘ **silme nuquerna (30)** This had the same meaning and sound as slime; 'nuquerna' means reversed. It may be used when there is a need to write a vowel sign above the *tengwa*.

ȣ **esse / áze (31)** Esse was the Quenya word for 'name' and had the sound 'z'. This *tengwa* also has the Quenya name áze meaning 'sunlight'.

ჳ esse nuquerna / áze nuquerna (32) This was the reversed form of esse and is used when there is need to write a vowel sign above the *tengwa*.

λ hyarmen (33) This was the Quenya word for 'south' and had the sound 'h'.

d hwesta sindarinwa (34) This was the Quenya word for 'Sindarin hwesta' and represented the sound 'w'.

Λ yanta (35) This was the Quenya word for 'bridge' and sometimes had the sound 'y'.

O úre (36) This was the Quenya word for 'heat' and had the sound 'w'.

Before we start writing with Tengwar, we need to know the language that is being written. Various languages, such as Quenya and Sindarin, may use different Tengwar letters for certain sounds. Some Tengwar letters represent the same sound in various languages, but others may represent different sounds in each language.

For example, if you are writing Quenya words then you need to understand what sounds in Quenya are represented by the Tengwar characters. For Sindarin or English, the sounds may be different. The set of tables below shows the sounds that the *tengwar* represent in Quenya, Sindarin and English.

Tengwar Table for Quenya

In Quenya the sounds that the *tengwar* represent as shown in Table 3 and Table 4.

	I		II		III		IV	
1	p	t	p	p	q	c/k	q	kw
2	pɔ	nd	p	mb	ccɋ	ng	ɋ	ngw
3	b	th/s	b	f	d	h	d	hw
4	bɔ	nt	bɔ	mp	cd	nk	cd	nkw
5	mɔ	n	m	m	cα	n	ɑɑ	nw
6	ɲ	r	ɲ	v	α	y	ɑ	v/w

Table 3: Tengwar for Quenya

ɣ	r	ɣ	rd	ᴄ	l	ᴢ	ld
6	s	ꝑ	l	ɠ	z, ss	ꝫ	z, ss
λ	h	d	ld	ʌ	y	ο	w

Table 4: Additional Tengwar for Quenya

Tengwar Table for Sindarin

In Sindarin the sounds that the *tengwar* represent as shown in Table 5 and Table 6.

	I		II		III		IV	
1		t		p		c		c/k
2		d		b		g		gw
3		th		f		ch		kh
4		dh		v		zh		gh
5		nn		mm		ny		ng
6		n		m		o		w

Table 5: Tengwar for Sindarin

	r		rh		l		lh
	s		y		ss		ss
	h		hw		e		u

Table 6: Additional Tengwar for Sindarin

Tengwar Table for English

Tengwar can also be used to represent sounds for English. Table 7 and Table 8 show a mapping from the *tengwar* to sounds that can be used for English. Note that there are variations in the mapping of sounds for English to the *tengwar*, however, this mapping is fairly widely used and is a good way to start.

1	p	t tea	p	p pie	q	ch chew	q	c/k kit
2	p	d dog	p	b big	q	j jam	q	g go
3	b	th three	b	f fig	d	sh she	d	kh loch
4	b	dh then	b	v vet	d	zh azure	d	gh aghast
5	m	n no	m	m mat	a	ny canyon	a	ng sing
6	n	r bar	n	w wet	a	y yet	a	-

Table 7: Tengwar for English

ʏ	r room	ʏ	rh rhesus	⊂	l live	ട	lh Delhi
6	s see	?	s see	૬	z zebra	૩	z zebra
λ	h he	௬	wh when	ʌ	-	o	-

Table 8: Additional Tengwar for English

Notice that both 's' and 'z' have two *tengwar* letters; either can be used depending on the need to place vowel marks above or below the letter. The placement of vowel marks will be described further in a later section.

Punctuation

Tengwar has the following symbols for punctuation.

comma	.
period	:
paragraph end	::
question mark	ß
exclamation mark	ς

Table 9: Tengwar Punctuation

Shortcuts

When writing English, Tolkien used some Tengwar letters as a shortcut way to represent whole words. Some of these Tengwar letters used a double-height stem which extended above and below the bow.

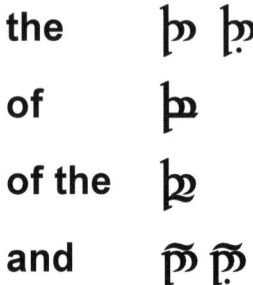

Table 10: Tengwar Shortcuts

Writing Tengwar Words

As mentioned before, writing using Tengwar depends on the language that is being written so that the *tengwa* that represents a particular sound can be selected. In addition, there are two modes for writing Tengwar:

- Mode of Beleriand or the Full Mode

- Traditional Mode or the Tehta Mode

The writing of Sindarin used both the Mode of Beleriand and the Traditional Mode, while writing of Quenya only used the Traditional Mode.

The Mode of Beleriand is somewhat easier so we will describe that first.

Mode of Beleriand

The Mode of Beleriand is also known as the Full Mode. This mode of writing Tengwar was used for the Sindarin language spoken by Grey Elves such as Legolas and Thranduil. Beleriand was the region of Middle Earth in which the Sindarin Elves of Doriath lived during the Second Age. Sindarin evolved from Quenya or High Elven during the First and Second Ages. The inscription on the Doors of Durin was written in Tengwar in the Mode of Beleriand.

To write Sindarin or English using the Mode of Beleriand you would first choose the *tengwa* from the Tengwar Table for Sindarin or the Tengwar Table for English.

In addition, in the Mode of Beleriand each vowel is assigned a *tengwa* as shown below.

a	e	i	o	u
c	Λ	I	α	o

Table 11: Vowels for the Mode of Beleriand

Let's start with the Sindarin word *mellon* which means 'friend'. It would be written like this:

ᴅᴧᴄᴄᴜᴅ

The Sindarin name for Gandalf was Mithrandir:

ᴅɪbɣᴄᴘ̃ɪɣ

Notice that the Tengwar letter **b** is used for 'th' in Mithrandir.

Table 12 provides a convenient reference to map letters from the English alphabet to the Tengwar for the Mode of Beleriand.

a	b	d	e	f	g	h	i	j	k	l	m
c	ᴘ	ᴘ	ᴧ	b	ᴄᴨ	λ	ɪ	ᴄᴨ	ᴨ	ᴄ	ᴍ

n	o	p	r	r final	s	t	u	v	w	y	z
ᴍ	ᴧ	ᴘ	ɣ	ᴅ	ó	ᴘ	o	ᴃ	ᴅ	ᴧ	ᴣ

ch	dh	gh	kh	ng	ny	sh	th	wh	zh
q	ᴃ	ᴆ	d	ᴃ	ᴃ	d	b	ᴅ	ᴃ

Table 12: English Tengwar Reference

You should now be able to read the Tengwar version of the title of this book written in the Mode of Beleriand.

þ ɒγιpιᴀ þ ᴄɒιɽᴢᴧ ᴧᴄγb

Rules

There are a few rules for writing Tengwar. These apply when writing both the Mode of Beleriand and the Traditional Mode.

1. A dot may be placed below a consonant for a silent 'e' that follows it.

   stone   ớpɑᴍ

2. The letter 'r' also has two *tengwar*, γ and ɒ. Their usage depends on the need for a harder 'r' sound or a softer 'r' sound as found at the end of a word. Use γ before vowels and ɒ before consonants and at the end of words. For example:

   red car   γᴧpᴍ qᴄɒ

3. To write a soft 'c' use the silme *tengwa*.

   cent   ớᴧᴍp

place   pˇcọ́

4. An underbar may be used with a consonant to double it. This permits some words to be written in two alternative ways, as shown below.

Pippin   pɪ̦ɪᴍ   pɪppɪᴍ

5. An overbar may be used with a consonant to indicate a preceding 'n' or 'm' sound. This allows two alternative ways of writing some words, as shown below.

find   bɪp̃   bɪᴍpᴑ

camp   qcp̃   qcᴍp

6. A curl or a hook may be appended to the last *tengwa* to add a plural 's'.

Hobbits   λɑp̦ɪp̦

Sindarin Names in the Mode of Beleriand

Here are Sindarin names written in the Mode of Beleriand using Tables 6, 7 and 11:

Amon Lhaw   cᴅɑᴑ ᶘcɑ

Arda   cypᴐc

Arwen   cyɑʌᴅ

Beleriand	ꝑᴧᴄᴧꝺɪᴄꝕ
Beren	ꝑᴧꝺᴧᴅ
Feanor	Ꮟᴧᴄᴅᴀꝺ
Fingolfin	ᏏɪꞷᴀᴄᏏɪᴅ
Glorfindel	ꞯᴄᴀꝺᏏɪꝕᴧᴄ
Gondolin	ꞯᴀꝕᴀᴄɪᴅ
Haldir	λᴄᴛꝑɪꝺ
Legolas	ᴄᴧꞯᴀᴄᴄᴓ
Lúthien	ᴄóᏏɪᴧᴅ
Silmaril	ᴓɪᴄᴅᴄꝺɪᴄ
Thingol	Ꮟɪꞷᴀᴄ
Thranduil	Ꮟꝺᴄꝕᴏɪᴄ

In the Mode of Beleriand, a vowel marking (or diacritic) called an *andaith* was used to indicate long or accented vowels. There is an example of this in the name 'Lúthien' above.

Some additional examples of *tengwar* used in the Mode of Beleriand are given in the following sections.

Inscription on the Doors of Durin

The inscription on the Doors of Durin is written in Sindarin using the Mode of Beleriand. This inscription reads as follows:

ᚪᛗᚷᚾ ᛈᚩᚤᛁᚾ ᚳᚤᚳᚾ ᚾᚪᚤᛁᚳ

Ennyn   Durin   Aran   Moria

Doors of Durin Lord of Moria

ᛈᚪᛈᚢ ᚾᚪᚳᚳᚢᚾ ᚳ ᚾᛁᛗᚢ

Pedo   mellon   a minno

Speak friend   and enter

ᛁᚾ ᚾᚳᚤᛒᛁ ᚦᚳᚾ ᚪᛞᚳᛈ :

Im   Narvi   hain   echant.

I   Narvi   them   made.

ᛲᚪᚳᚪᛗᚤᛁᛈᚢᚤ ᚢ ᚪᚤᚪᛩᛁᚢᚾ

Celebrimbor	o Eregion
Celebrimbor	of Hollin

pӒbcp̃ ꞁ bιɑ λꝑ :

teithant I thiw hin.

drew   these signs.

Note the use of the overbar in the words 'echant',
'Celebrimbor', and 'teithant' to indicate the nasal 'n' and 'm',
respectively.

The complete inscription is then 'The Doors of Durin, Lord of
Moria. Speak, friend, and enter. I, Narvi, made them.
Celebrimbor of Hollin drew these signs'.

Elbereth Gilthoniel

Elbereth Gilthoniel, also known as the Hymn of Imladris, is a
poem written to Varda, one of the heavenly creatures of the
First Age. This poem was set to music in a collaboration
between Tolkien and the composer Donald Swann. This verse
can be found in their song cycle 'The Road Goes Ever On',
published in 1967. This poem is in Sindarin, written in the
Mode of Beleriand.

c ʌʨꟼʌγʌb ᴡɪʨbɑᴅιʌʨ

A Elbereth   Gilthoniel

45

O Elbereth   Star-kindler

ótiɪɓ yʌɒ pʌɒc ɒíɣɪʌ

silivren   penna míriel

white-glittering, slanting down

sparkling like a jewel

c ɒʌɒʌc cɯ̨ccɣ ʌcʌɒcɒ

O menel   aglar   elenath!

from [the] firmament [the]

glory [of] the star-host!

ɒċ dcʌɣʌɒ pccɒ píɣɪʌc

Na-chaered   palan-díriel

to remote distance far-having gazed

ɑ ɯ̨cccɒ yʌ ɒ ɪɒ ʌɒ ɑ ycɒ

o galadhremmin   ennorath,

from [the] tree-tangled middle-lands,

bcnöʒuɓ ʒʌ ʒɪɱcbʋɒ

Fanuilos,   le   linnathon

Fanuilos, to thee I will chant

ɒʌɓ cʌcy ɓí ɒʌɓ cʌcyʋɒ :

nef   aear, sí nef   aearon!

on this side of the ocean, here

on this side of the Great Ocean!

Traditional or Tehta Mode

To write Quenya using the Tehta Mode you would first select the Tengwar letters from the Tengwar Table (Tables 3 and 4) for Quenya.

Unlike the Mode of Beleriand, the Traditional Mode does not have vowel characters but instead uses special vowel markings (or diacritics) called *tehtar* that are placed just above consonants. The singular of *tehtar* is *tehta*. If there is no consonant available at the right position in a word, then a vowel-carrier is used for the vowel. There is a short vowel carrier **I** and a long vowel-carrier **ʃ**.

The *tehtar* used to represent the vowels are listed below as if they were placed on the short vowel-carrier.

a	e	i	o	u
i̊	í	i̇	î	i̓

Table 13: Tehtar - short vowels

For a long vowel, the vowel mark is placed on the long vowel-carrier.

ā	ē	ī	Ō	ū
j̊	j́	j̇	ĵ	j̓

Table 14: Tehtar - long vowels

The final 'y' of a word is represented with this *tehta* on a vowel-carrier.

y   ǐ

Tengwar also uses these *tengwar*, **Λ**, **O**, and **Ⴉ**, combined with *tehtar* to represent diphthongs.

ai	ei	oi	ui	au	eu	ou
Λ̊	Λ́	Λ̂	Λ̓	o̊	ó	ô

Table 15: Tehtar for Diphthongs I

Here are sample words using these diphthongs.

pain	p̊ⱉ
rein	yⱉ
point	p̂ⱉp
cruise	qyⱉ́
daub	p̊ⱉ
feud	ɓópⱉ
pout	póp

ay	ey	oy	uy
å	á	â	å

Table 16: Tehtar for Diphthongs II

Here are sample words using these diphthongs.

day	p̊å
they	ɓá
boy	p̊â

buy   ᵽʊá

There are two methods of placing a *tehta* vowel mark on a consonant, depending on what language the Tengwar is being used to write.

- Following placement, where the vowel mark is placed on the following consonant.

- Preceding placement, where the vowel mark is placed on the preceding consonant.

Preceding Placement

When writing Quenya and other languages such as French or Spanish in which words often end with vowels, the *tehta* is placed on the consonant that precedes the vowel. The script is written in a zig-zag fashion, with each vowel *tehta* being written above the preceding consonant.

The Quenya word *tengwar* would therefore be written in the order shown below in Figure 1.

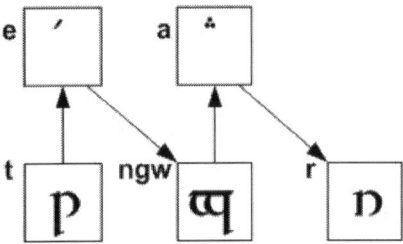

Figure 1: Preceding Placement

The result appears below. Notice that **ᴄ** is used for 'ngw' in *tengwar*.

ᵖᶜᵖᵈ

If there is no preceding consonant, as at the beginning of a word, then the vowel carrier **ɪ** is used as shown for the Quenya word for 'star' *elen*:

ɪᶜᵈᵈ

Following Placement

When writing Sindarin, Black Speech, or English, the *tehta* is placed on the consonant that follows the vowel. The English word 'return' would be written with the *tehtar* placed over the following *tengwar* in the order shown below in Figure 2.

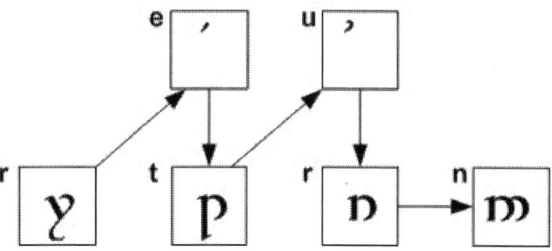

Figure 2: Following Placement

So 'return' is written with following placement as

Tehta Rules

There are a few additional rules for writing in the Tehta Mode.

1. If there is a silent vowel, then a dot is placed below the preceding consonant. To write the English word 'here', use following placement and then add a dot below the 'r' for the final silent 'e':

here   λý

2. For doubled vowels, each *tehta* may be placed on its own vowel carrier, or they may be placed together on a consonant.

book   ꝑíïꝗ   ꝑꝗ̃

keep   ꝗíïꝑ   ꝗꝑ̃

3. If there is an accent on a vowel then the *tehta* is placed on a separate long vowel-carrier **|**, as shown below in

Lúthien, written with preceding placement. Note that the Tengwar letter  is used for 'th' in Lúthien.

Lúthien 

Here is the title of this book written in the Tehta Mode using following placement of vowel marks.

Elvish Names in the Tehta Mode

Here are some well-known Elvish names from *The Lord of the Rings*. These Quenya words use the *tengwar* from Tables 3 and 4 and all the *tehtar* are placed over the preceding *tengwar*.

Amon Lhaw 

Arda 

Beleriand 

Beren 

Elessar 

Feanor 

Fingolfin	bɑ́ɟȼƀɯ
Finwe	bɯɑ́
Gondolin	ɑ́ɯᵽ̂ȼɯ
Noldor	ɯ̂ȼᵽ̂ɯ
Numenor	ɯ̂ɯ̃ɯ̂ɯ
Silmaril	ʒȼɯ̃ẏ̇ȼ
Thingol	bɑ̂ȼ
Valinor	ɑ̊ȼɯ̂ɯ
Varda	ɑ̊ẏ̊

English Words in Tengwar

Here are some English words written using *tengwar* from Tables 7 and 8 in the Tehta Mode with all the *tehtar* placed over the following *tengwar*. Note the use of the vowel-carrier where there are two adjacent vowels or there is a vowel at the end of a word.

| apple | p̊ȼ |
| are | ẙ̊ |

case	ꝗő
children	ꝗꞇꝓꝩꝥ
city	ɕꝑĭ
Daniel	ꝓꝳïꞇ
Eileen	ʌꞇíꝥ
elvish	ꞇbɑd
England	ꝏꞇꝥꝓ
gnomes	ꝗꝓꝏ
hope	λꝑ
Julie	ꞃꝗꞇi
king	ꝗꝏ
love	ꞇbő
nine	ꝓꝓ
people	píꝑꞇ
red	ꝩꝑ
Richard	ꝩꝗꝥꝓ

robin	ᴙᴘᵐᵐ
script	ᴕᴄᴙᴘᴘ
see	ᴕíí
Sheila	ᴅɪᴄᴉ
slow	ᴕᴄᴥ
speech	ᴕᴘᴼ
Theo	ᴃíí
this	ᴃᴐᴐ
very	ᴃᴥᴋᴉ
wish	ᴅᴅ
world	ᴅᴐᴄᴘ

Use these examples to write your own name in Tengwar in the Tehta Mode.

Tengwar Fonts

There are many Tengwar fonts available on the Internet. A later chapter will describe how to download them. Here are samples of these fonts. Links to these fonts are provided in the Further Reading chapter.

Tengwar Quenya by Daniel Smith

Tengwar Sindarin by Daniel Smith

Tengwar Noldor by Daniel Smith

Tengwar Annatar by Johan Winge

Tengwar Naive by Johan Winge

Tengwar Parmaite by Måns Björkman

Tengwar Eldamar by Måns Björkman

Tengwar Cursive by Harri Perälä

Tengwar Typewriter by Jeff Anderson

Tengwar Elfica by Enrique Mombello

Tengwar Hereno by Paulo Alberto Otto

Tengwar Formal by Michal Nowakowski

Tengwar Tellepsalinnacontar by 'Tencedil'

Elfetica by Ronald Kyrmse

The Lord of the Rings Title Page

The Lord of the Rings title page shows English sentences transliterated into Quenya Tengwar by placing the *tehtar* above the following *tengwar*.

Of West March

bɪ ɷλɳ́ yɳ́ċ̇ɒ ýíí̇ẻ p̊ċ̇qiɳ́ :

by John Ronald Reuel Tolkien.

λ̇ýɳ́ ϟ 6ṕ bɳ́b ꝑ λ6pɣ̈ĭ

Herein is set forth the history

ꝑ   ɒɳ́ ꝑ   yɷ̇ɪ

of the War of the Ring

p̃   ꝑ yṕɒ̀ɳ ꝑ   qɷ̇ɪ

and the Return of the King

ꝫ̇ 6íɪɳ bɪ ꝑ λꝑ̈p̈ :

as seen by the Hobbits.

59

Ring Inscription

The inscription on the One Ring is in the Black Speech that was invented by Sauron. It appears in Chapter 2, 'The Shadow of the Past', in *The Fellowship of the Ring*. It was written in Tengwar, as shown below in Johan Winge's Tengwar Annatar font.

As this is Black Speech the *tehtar* are placed over the following *tengwar*. Also note that for 'u' vowels a forward-curl *tehta* is used instead of the usual reverse-curl *tehta*. There are two forward-curl *tehtar* placed over consonants in the words 'durbatulûk' and 'thrakatulûk' to represent the accented 'û'.

Ash nazg   durbatulûk

One ring to rule them all,

ash nazg   gimbatul

one ring to find them,

Ash nazg   thrakatulûk
One ring to bring them all

agh burzum-ishi krimpatul.
and in the darkness bind them.

There is no word separation in the script that appears in *The Fellowship of the Ring*.

There are also other fonts such as Tengwar Cursive that can be used.

Námarië

Námarië (meaning 'Farewell') is Tolkien's well-known poem that was set to music in the collaboration with Donald Swann called 'The Road Goes Ever On'. This is in Quenya with the *tehtar* in preceding placement. Here are the first lines of Námarië.

Ai! laurië lantar lassi súrinen,

Ah! like the gold fall the leaves in the wind,

yéni ve lintë yuldat avánier

the long years have passed

like swift draughts

ᶂᶄᶆᶇ ᶈᶉᶊᶋᶌ ᶍ ᶎᶏᶐᶑ ᶒᶓᶔᶕᶖ

yéni únótimë ve rámar aldaron!

long years numberless as the

wings of trees!

ᶗᶘ ᶙᶚᶛᶜ ᶝᶞ ᶟᶠᶡᶢᶣ

mi oromardi lissë-miruvóreva

of the sweet mead in lofty halls

ᶤᶥᶦᶧ ᶨᶩ ᶪᶫ ᶬᶭᶮᶯ

Andúnë pella, Vardo tellumar

beyond the West, beneath the

blue vaults of Varda

ᶰ ᶱᶲᶳ ᶴᶵᶶ ᶷᶸᶹᶺ ᶻ ᶼᶽᶾ

nu luini yassen tintilar i eleni

wherein the stars tremble

ĵɯĵŷ Λ́ŷpĵṗ ꞇĵŷɱ́ɱ

ómaryo airetári-lírinen.

in the voice of her song, holy and queenly.

Tengwar Numbers

Tengwar has a set of characters for numbers. The characters and their names are listed below.

0	munta	ɔ
1	mine	ꞇ
2	atta	ꞇ
3	nelde	ꞇꞇ
4	canta	l
5	lempe	ꞇ
6	enque	ꞇꞇ

7	otso	]
8	tolto	þ
9	nerte	þ
10	cainen	ა
11	minque	ვ

To make the Tengwar numbers more clearly distinct from letters, a dot was placed above each digit. Tengwar numbers are written with the least-significant number placed on the left, as shown below:

10 → 01 → ɔ̇ċ

11 → 11 → ċċ

1952 → 2591 → ɔ̇ċ þ̇ɔ̇ċ

Some of the Elves also used a duo-decimal (base-12) numbering system, which employed the characters ა and ვ to represent the numbers 10 and 11. In duo-decimal numbering, the numbers 10 and 11 are usually represented as A and B, so the duo-decimal number $1B_{12}$ has the same value as the decimal number 23_{10}:

$1B = 1 \times 12^1 + 11 \times 12^0 = 12 + 11 = 23$

The duo-decimal Tengwar numbers were also written with the least-significant number placed on the left, with a dot or a line placed below each digit. The duo-decimal number 23 would be written as:

23 → **32** → ꚍꚍ

Sometimes a small circle was placed under the least significant digit instead of the dot.

23 → **32** → ꚍꚍ

Here is the sequence of duo-decimal numbers from decimal 9 to decimal 15.

9	10	11	12	13	14	15
9	A	B	10	11	12	13

ꝑ ꝺ ꝺ Ꝼ Ꝼꝼ ꝼꝼ ꝼꝼ

Using Rune Fonts on a Computer

Computer Fonts

Now we are going to find out how to write runes on your computer. This can be done using a word processor such as Microsoft Word on a PC or a Mac.

Start Word. On the Word toolbar you will see the currently active font, which is probably Arial or Times New Roman. Type some text and select that text. Next, click on the drop-down box for the font selector and you will see a list of fonts. Choose a different font and see that your text changes to appear in the new font. Now you will need to download rune fonts from the Internet, as described in the next section.

Downloading and Installing Fonts

Various rune fonts can be downloaded from the Internet. A good Web site for rune fonts is Dan Smith's Fantasy Fonts for Windows at www.acondia.com/fonts. On the main Web page you will see links to the three fonts described in this book:

- Hobbit fonts

- Cirth fonts

- Tengwar fonts

Look for the links to download these fonts for Windows or the Mac. Click on the link for the font you need and then download that font to your computer.

Once downloaded, the font file will be in the Downloads folder. You need to unzip the font file. When this is done on a PC, you will see the font file with an Install button as shown below. Click on it to install the font. The font will be installed on your computer and is available for you to use. You will need to restart Word or any other application so that it can use the rune font that you have just installed.

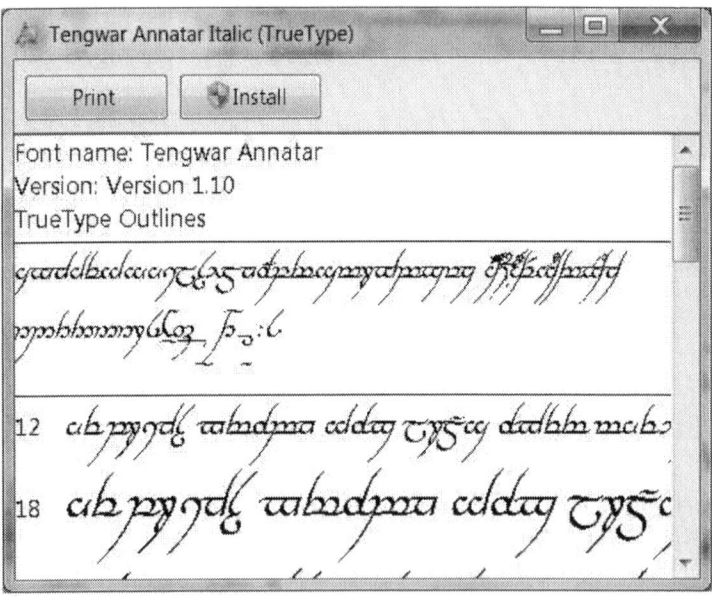

On the Mac you need to open Font Book, then click on File, followed by Add Font. Next, find and select the font that you have just downloaded from the Downloads folder. Font Book will then install the font on your Mac.

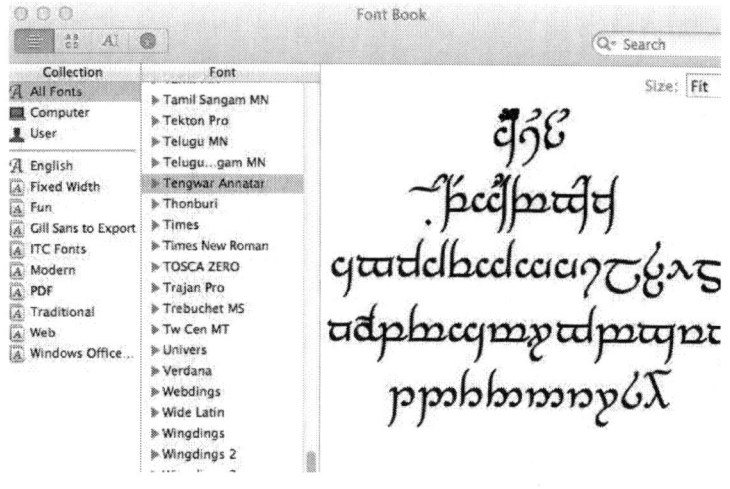

Using Rune Fonts

To use the fonts in Word, click on the font selector box and scroll down to find the rune font you want to use. Now, as you type text you should see runes of the selected font appear in the document.

The next thing you need to do is work out how the keyboard maps to the runes. The rune fonts you download are likely to have different schemes for mapping from the keyboard to the actual rune. This mapping is usually described in a 'readme' file that is included with the font download.

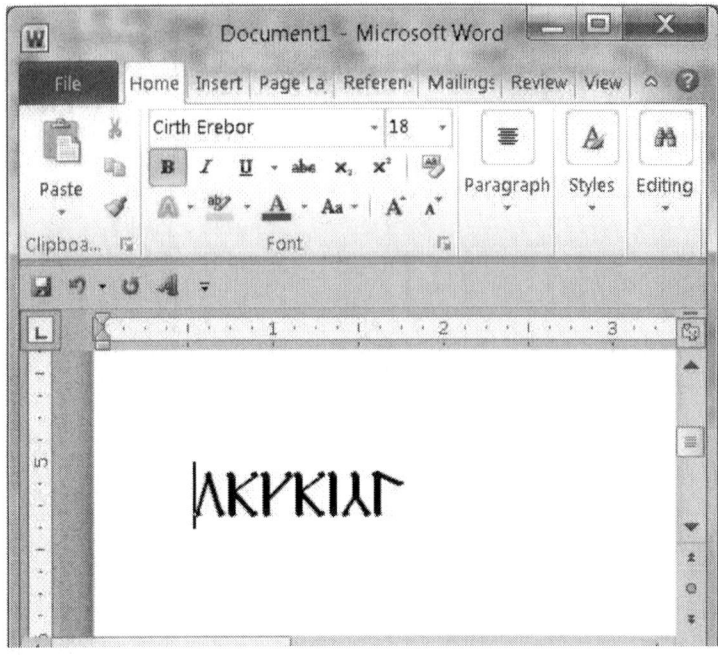

Hobbit Runes

For Dan Smith's Hobbit Runes, select Dwarf Runes from the font drop-down menu. Hobbit runes have a straightforward mapping from the computer keys to the rune characters that matches the Hobbit Rune Table in the Hobbit Rune Chapter. As you type, you will get the correct rune for each key.

Cirth

Select the Cirth font, such as Cirth Erebor, from the font drop-down menu. The mapping of the computer keys to Cirth runes is described in the file 'CirthErebor_Help' that is included in the Cirth zip-file that you downloaded. You will find a keyboard layout showing the mapping of the keys to Cirth runes. To write in Cirth, press the keys that correspond to the Cirth runes that you want to write. In Word you can also click on Insert, followed by Symbol, to insert a character. The popup Symbol menu will appear as shown below. You can then select the rune that you want to insert.

Tengwar

Select the Tengwar font such as Dan Smith's Tengwar Quenya from the font drop-down menu. The mapping of the computer keys to Tengwar is described in the file 'TengwarKeyMap' that is included in the Tengwar zip file that you downloaded. You will find keyboard layout showing the mapping of the keys to Tengwar. To write in Tengwar, press the keys that correspond to the Tengwar characters that you want to write. In Word you can also click on Insert followed by Symbol to insert a character. Select the *tengwa* from the popup Symbol menu.

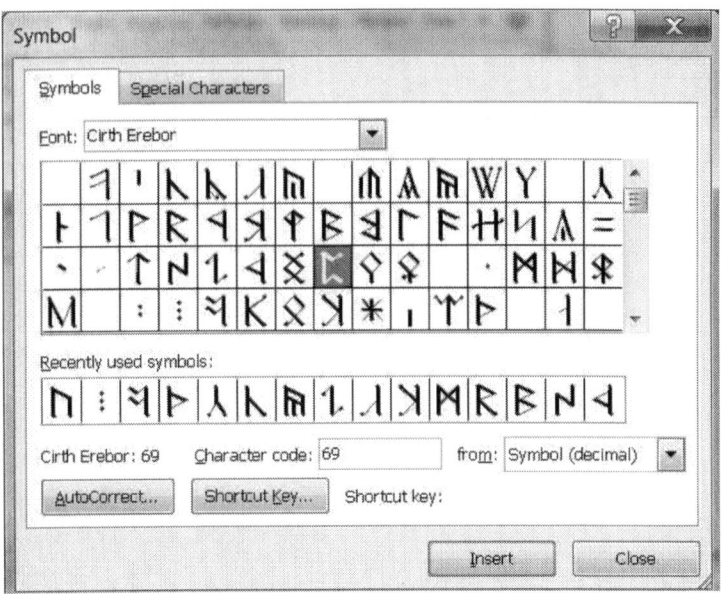

Writing Using the Tehta Mode

First select the Tengwar font. Next you need to decide whether you are going to use forward placement or preceding placement of the *tehtar*. This will depend on what language you are going to write. For writing English or Sindarin, following placement is typically used, and for writing Quenya, preceding placement is used.

Choose the consonant above which the *tehta* is to be placed. Type that consonant and then type the key for the *tehta* that you want to use. Here is an example of forward placement in writing the word 'dog', where the 'o' vowel is placed atop the 'g'. Type the key for the 𝕡 and then the key for the 𝕢, and finally type the key for the *tehta* Ô to insert it above the 𝕢.

d → 𝕡

g → 𝕡𝕢

o → 𝕡𝕢́

Here is another example with forward placement as well as indication of the final silent vowel below a consonant. To write the word 'are', first type the 𝕪. Next insert the *tehta* Ö above the 𝕪. Finally, insert the dot that represents the final silent 'e'.

r → 𝕪

a → 𝕪̈

e → 𝕪̈

It is also possible to insert more than one vowel mark above a consonant. Use these steps to write the Tengwar in the Tehta Mode.

Quiz

Here is a quiz with various types of writing that you can try to decipher. The answers are at the back of the book. Have fun!

Quiz 1

ᚦᛖ · ᛞᛗᚢᛖᛋᚠᛏᛁᛖᛏ · ᚠᚹ · ᚢᛗᚠᚾᚷ

Quiz 2

᛬ᚢᚻ᛫ᚦᚻᛏᛏᛅᚩᛅᛁᛈ᛫ᛚᚦ᛫ᚻᛏᚢᚻᚲ᛫ᚾᚷ᛫ᚠᚩᚾᛏᚢᚻᚲ᛬

Quiz 3

þ yucꝧ ꞇꞅuʌ6 ʌꞵꞵʌꞃ uꝳ

Quiz 4

Quiz 5

Quiz 6

Quiz 7

Quiz 8

Quiz 9

Quiz 10

ħýíí ϭpïc͜ ̄ þ ċbɔd ϭqnþp

Quiz 11

λbb̈ ̇ï bɔýĭ λp̈ï qnϭpɯ̌ö

.

Answers

Here are the answers to the Quiz.

Bilbo's Riddle (Hobbit Runes, from page 11)

ᚠ· ᛒᚠᛦ·ᛈᛁᛏᚾᚠᚾᛏ·ᚾᛁᛏᚷᛗᛘ·ᚺᛗᛗ·ᚠᚱ·ᚱᛁᚾ·
A box without hinges key or lid

ᛘᛗᛏ·ᚷᚠᛏᛗᛗᛏ·ᛏᚱᛗᚠᛙᚾᚱᛗ·ᛁᛏᛙᛁᚾᛗ· ᛁᛙ·ᚾᛁᚾ⁞
yet golden treasure   inside is hid.

Quiz 1 Hobbit Runes

ᚦᛗ · ᛗᛗᛙᚠᛏᚠᛏᛁᚠᛏ · ᚠᛦ · ᛙᛗᚠᚾᚷ
The Desolation   of   Smaug

Quiz 2 Angerthas Erebor Cirth

⁞�155ᚻ·ᚻᛙᛏᛏᛣ156ᛣᛁᛈ·ᚵᚻ·ᚾᛏᛣᚻᚲ·ᛙᚷ·ᚠᚦᛏᛣᚻᚲ⁞
The Fellowship of Elves   and Dwarves

Quiz 3 Tengwar in Tehta Mode with following placement

The road   goes   ever   on

Quiz 4 Tengwar in Tehta Mode with following placement

One   ring to rule them   all

Quiz 5 Tengwar in Tehta Mode with following placement

I sit   beside the fire and think

Quiz 6 Runes of Gondolin

The wedding of Tuor and Idril

Quiz 7 Tengwar in Tehta Mode with following placement

The lost road into the west

Quiz 8 Tengwar in Tehta Mode with following placement

The Elves of the lonely   Isle

Quiz 9 Tengwar in Tehta Mode with following placement

The tale of the downfall   of   Númenor

Quiz 10 Tengwar in Tehta Mode with following placement

Three styles   of Elvish script

Quiz 11 Tengwar in Tehta Mode with following placement

Have a very   happy Christmas

Further Reading

Books

- *An Introduction to Elvish*, Jim Allan
- *The Fellowship of the Ring* (1954) - Houghton Mifflin
- *The Two Towers* (1954) - Houghton Mifflin
- *The Return of the King* (1955) - Houghton Mifflin
- *The Road Goes Ever On* (1967 & 1978) - Houghton Mifflin
- *The Silmarillion* (1977) - Houghton Mifflin
- *Pictures by J.R.R. Tolkien* (1979) - Houghton Mifflin
- *Pictures by J.R.R. Tolkien* (1992) revised edition - Houghton Mifflin
- *Unfinished Tales* (1980) - Houghton Mifflin
- *The Letters of J.R.R. Tolkien* (1981) - Houghton Mifflin
- *The History of Middle-earth I* - The Book of Lost Tales, Part One (1984) - Houghton Mifflin
- *The History of Middle-earth II - The Book of Lost Tales*, Part Two (1984) - Houghton Mifflin
- *The History of Middle-earth III - The Lays of Beleriand* (1985) - Houghton Mifflin
- *The History of Middle-earth IV - The Shaping of Middle-earth* (1986) - Houghton Mifflin
- *The History of Middle-earth V - The Lost Road* (1987) - Houghton Mifflin
- *The History of Middle-earth VI - The Return of the Shadow* (1988) - Houghton Mifflin

- *The History of Middle-earth VII - The Treason of Isengard* (1989) - Houghton Mifflin
- *The History of Middle-earth VIII - The War of the Ring* (1990) - Houghton Mifflin
- *The History of Middle-earth IX - Sauron Defeated* (1992) - Houghton Mifflin
- *The History of Middle-earth X - Morgoth's Ring* (1993) - Houghton Mifflin
- *The History of Middle-earth XI - The War of the Jewels* (1994) - Houghton Mifflin
- *The History of Middle-earth XII - The Peoples of Middle-earth* (1996) - Houghton Mifflin

Web Sites

- Dan Smith's Fantasy Fonts for Windows **www.acondia.com/fonts**
- Fontspace **http://www.fontspace.com/category/tengwar**
- DaFont.com

  http://www.dafont.com/tengwar-annatar.font
- Free Tengwar Font Project

  http://freetengwar.sourceforge.net/
- The Mythopoeic Society **http://www.mythsoc.org/**

Printed in Great Britain
by Amazon

47561180R00048